Table of Contents

D1607909

DEDICATION

To

Being seen may be the only way to truly know who you are.

PROLOGUE

There was a time when I thought that moving from place to place every few months was the life. I never stayed anywhere for more than a few months. What was the point? I didn't care about these people or their lives. Why should I? No one ever really gave a shit about me, or at least they hadn't in years. When the people in whatever town I was currently staying got to know me too well, it was time to get the hell out. I was good at being alone. Being the dependable guy everyone relied on was a role I would never play again. The minute my parents kicked me out of the house was the moment I stopped being the nice guy. At first, most of it was an act, but the longer I pretended to be the bad boy, the less of an imagination it took and the more real it became.

CHAPTER 1

"Fuck!"

This kind of shit always happened to me. Having to fix my bike so long on my own I knew exactly what the problem was, unfortunately it wasn't something I could fix on the side of the road. From the signs a few miles back, the next town was probably six to seven miles ahead. I had a choice, either I could leave the bike and hope it was still there when I got back or I could push it all the way into town and find a place to fix it there.

The thought of leaving the only thing I cared about on the side of the road didn't really sit well with me. Sighing, I pulled off the jacket I was wearing. It wasn't hot on the bike with the breeze blowing, but walking with the sun beating down was an entirely different story. I stored the jacket in the saddlebag. With a groan I stood the bike up and started the long walk. Pushing the bike that far was not going to be easy. My original plan had been to go much farther west, closer to the city. For now this town was just going to have to do.

After about twenty minutes, the sweat was sliding down my face onto my neck. The sun was much hotter than I thought it would be on the empty stretch of road. Traveling from place to place killed my desire to ride on the highways. People drove like assholes most of the time. It was especially bad when they were anywhere in the vicinity of a motorcycle. Drivers always fell into one of two categories. They were either idiots who wanted to race you or fools who slowed down to a ridiculous speed, way below the speed limit in some stupid ass fear that you were going to drive dangerously and get yourself killed.

The back roads, such as the one I was on, were usually the best bet. Not much traffic and the few people that you did see on the road ignored you. The only problem with the lack of highway was when shit like this happened, no one else was around for miles. My fucked up luck combined with the empty roadway had made for a pretty crappy day.

Hunched over, pushing the bike was sending pains down my back. Unfortunately, I still had a long way to go and no other options. That's when I heard the rumbling in the distance. It was definitely a truck of some kind, but with the loud popping coming from the transmission, it didn't sound to be in that great of shape.

When the old Chevy pickup passed me without even slowing down, I wasn't really surprised. Not many people wanted to stop and help out a guy with a bike. Everyone was afraid of the big, bad biker. The stereotypical bullshit made me crazy. In my opinion, people watched a little too much TV.

The brake lights went on as the truck jerked to a stop about five hundred feet in front of me. When the reverse lights came on, I braced myself for whatever reaction came from the driver. Taking the bike out of the equation, the fact that tattoos ran down both of my arms usually made people a little wary of me.

"Hey, man, need a lift?" the driver asked, leaning across the cab of the truck to yell out the passenger window. He was covered in tats of his own. From the looks of him, he was probably about my size, a little over 6'2" when standing.

"I'd love one, but I don't want to leave her on the side of the road."

He smiled. "I don't blame you, man. Come on, we'll toss her in the back of the truck and take her to my shop in town. We can see if we can get her running again."

That sounded like exactly what I needed after the day I had. "Thanks." If he wasn't going to be intimidated by me, I wasn't going to turn down a perfectly good offer of help.

The driver pulled up on the side of the road in front of me, jumping out, he came around the back and held his hand out to me. "I'm Kaden, by the way." I took his hand.

"Ryder."

Leaning up into the bed of the truck, he pulled out a few boards we could use as a ramp to push the bike up into the truck. He walked over and did a quick once over of my bike, before grabbing the handle bars. "Damn. This baby's nice."

"Thanks."

With Kaden at the bars, while I pushed from the rear of the bike, we managed to get it into the back of the truck and tied down in no time. When we were both settled in the cab, he turned to me. "Do you know what might be wrong with it?"

"Yeah, I'm pretty sure the fuel line is clogged."

"I don't usually carry a lot of bike parts in my shop, not a huge need for them around here, but if I don't have it I can order it."

Damn that was all I needed. I really didn't feel like waiting for a part to come in. "Figures," I mumbled under my breath. I might have been frustrated but I didn't want to insult the guy who was offering to get what I needed. "That would be awesome."

Kaden faced forward and started towards the town. Silence filled the cab at first, which was fine with me, I had no interest in making small talk. Not that it lasted. Apparently Kaden wasn't someone who preferred the quiet, or at least that was my best guess. It wasn't like I could ignore him, he was trying to help me out of a really shitty situation.

"Did you plan on staying in town, or were you just passing through?"

"I was supposed to be passing through, but I guess I'm might have to stay now. Is there a motel in town?"

"Yeah, not too bad a place either."

"Well, if I have to, I'll grab a room there."

"Alright man. We'll run by the shop first in case I do have the part. If not, I'll drop you by the motel in town."

"Thanks for the help."

"No problem. It's way too fucking hot to be pushing a bike that heavy."

"You're telling me," I said with a chuckle.

The minute we drove into town, I could sense the small town feel of the place. Not small in size, but a place where everyone knew everyone else, even if you wished they didn't. These types of towns were never a good place to be, especially for a loner like me. Trouble always seemed to find people like me in places like that. It was easier to blend in when the people you dealt with didn't always remember you, or should I say care to remember.

Pulling up in front of a small, run down garage, I knew by the looks of the place, there was no way he was going to have the part I needed in stock. The ten or so cars out front were a testament to who his normal clients were.

"Let's get her in the garage and I'll see what I have."

Nodding, I stepped out of the cab and walked to the back of the truck. We rolled the bike down a ramp Kaden had grabbed from inside the garage and I pushed it into the now open door. It only took Kaden a few minutes to look through the parts he had in stock for motorcycles. Even from the inside it looked like this garage worked on cars more than anything else. Just like I figured, he didn't have the right one.

"Sorry, man, I can have it here in a few days."

"Not a problem. I'll pay for it now."

"Don't worry about it. We'll deal with it when it comes in. Just give me a minute." He typed away on his computer. "All right that should take care of it. Why don't you give me your number? That way I can get in touch with you when it gets here and then I'll take you over to the motel in town."

I wrote my number down on a sheet of paper. "Are you sure you don't mind keeping the bike here?"

"Not at all. It's actually easier than lugging it to and from the motel when the part comes in."

I reached out to shake his hand. "Thanks, I'd have been stuck today if you wouldn't have stopped."

"Not a problem. I'm glad I could help."

"Let me just grab my stuff and I'll be ready to head on over." I pulled the saddle bags off the back and looked around for Kaden. The beat up Chevy was still sitting out front of the garage, but it was empty. The purring of a sports car hit my ears, before the car pulled around the corner. It was a gorgeous 1969 Camaro that looked completely rebuilt to the original specs.

"Holy shit, man, this is a nice car." My eyes flicked between the truck and the beautiful piece of machinery in front of me.

Afraid to touch the door, or any part of the car for that matter, I carefully lifted the handle and opened the door. Kaden laughed.

"You won't hurt her, Ryder. I drive her all the time. The Chevy is the piece of shit I use to haul crap out to the junkyard. If I drove that thing around no one would ever trust me to fix their cars."

I laughed. "Good point."

He put the car in gear and pulled out of the lot.

"What is there to do here?" I asked.

"There's a couple of good places to eat right near the motel, but I'd suggest *Ryan's*. It's within walking distance, about two blocks down the road."

"They don't happen to have a bar do they? I could use a drink or two after the day I've had."

"There is a bar and great food."

The drive to the motel was quick, less than five minutes. It looked a bit run down. Then again, based on the age of the rest of the town, it looked no worse for the wear and as long as it had clean sheets and a shower, that was all I really needed anyway.

After a quick check-in, and a once over by the woman behind the counter, like I was going to destroy the place or steal every dollar in her register, I went up to the room to drop my bag. The sweat from earlier still stuck to my skin like an uncomfortable shirt. I needed a shower and food. Once that was taken care of, I could focus on what I was going to do when I finally reached the city.

Part of me was getting tired of the constant moving, but I couldn't deny the desire to keep my privacy, something you didn't get in the small towns I lived in so far. The only time having company was worth it was when you had a beautiful naked woman in your bed. If you didn't, you were better off on your own. It was the main reason I was heading for a larger city this time. Getting lost in the shuffle should be fairly easy and it should keep me from having to move again.

Being in a town like this wasn't that unusual for me. Over the last few years, I stayed in my fair share of small towns.

They were the ones I never stayed in long. Someone always wanted to whisper about the biker guy who kept to himself. Not that people's opinion bothered me, shit for all I cared they could shove their opinion right up their ass.

No it wasn't those people, it was the morons who were brave enough to talk about the gossip to your face. That kinda crap always sent me over the edge. I ended up in more fights than I could count, over some small minded dipshit making comments about me that just weren't true. If they only knew my actual name and where I came from, they'd probably keep their mouths shut. Then again, I'd also probably be in jail for something worse than a bar brawl, even if I had nothing to do with it.

Shaking my head, I tried to clear my thoughts. Dwelling on the past was not going to fix anything. If I was going to settle down in one place, I was going to have to get it together and stop letting the stupid shit bother me.

Maybe if it wasn't for my temper, I'd have stayed with my parents. Going to college where they wanted me to and thanking my lucky stars that they paid the bill while I used my time to party. Maybe they would have believed me when I told them the truth. But there was no going back. It didn't help that my father's temper was as bad, if not worse, than mine. Who was I kidding, they would never believe me. Things were said that could never be taken back.

Growing up, my father and I had not been particularly close. It wasn't the type of relationship many kids complain about where their father treats them like crap. He was a great father, it more had to do with the fact that we didn't have a lot of the same interests.

My brother, David and I had more in common than we did with my dad. Dad liked baseball, we preferred football. We were almost inseparable, even though he was a year younger than me. The only time we were really apart before I left for college was once we reached high school, but we sat together with all of our friends at lunch.

The problems started my first year of college. In the beginning, we talked all of the time. But slowly as the months passed, the texts and phone calls between us became less and less. School was crazy, but I would always have time for my brother.

Then when I came home for winter break that first year, David was standoffish, almost as if he didn't want to be around me. Slowly, we began talking again, but it wasn't the same and the minute I left for school again, I stopped hearing from him all together. As hard as I tried, I could never find out what happened between the two of us. After that he avoided me all together.

Fuck. Thinking about that day always got me riled up. This was my life now and I was going to do my best to live it the way I wanted.

A shower. That's what I needed. It would help me clear my mind and focus on the present. Standing up I rooted through my bag to grab what I needed and made my way into the bathroom.

Stepping into the warm shower, I washed all of the sweat from my body, then stood under the spray until the water began to run cold. The frigid temperature of the water forced me from my sanctuary and out into the room to get dressed. With my mind relaxed and cleared I was able to focus on the next thing, which was food.

Kaden had mentioned a place called *Ryan's* as being one of the best in town. I figured what the hell. It couldn't hurt to try and since they had beer on tap, it sounded like the perfect place for me. I threw on a pair of jeans, my boots, a black t-shirt, and walked out the door.

Just like Kaden had said, it was only about two blocks and a pretty quick walk from the motel. One look and it was clear that this place didn't necessarily belong in a town like this. Yet something told me that it was the perfect place for me at the moment.

CHAPTER 2

Sitting down at the bar, I noticed the place wasn't very crowded. I had a feeling that wouldn't last very long, especially with the way Kaden talked about the food. The room was set up in a way that would keep the diners and the bar patrons separate. There were tables and booths at one end of the room, with a bar in the middle, and pool tables at the other end. The bar seemed like the perfect spot. Seeing how my day had gone so far, I was definitely going to need a couple of beers, if not a shot or two.

Not long after I sat down, a hot ass brunette came over to take my order. The black V-neck she was wearing cut low enough to give me a glimpse of the most gorgeous set of tits I'd seen in years. The kind you wanted to use as a pillow after a marathon round of sex. There was a snap in front of my face, breaking me out of my day dream. I let the lazy grin that made the girls wet their panties, spread across my face.

"Nice try buddy that 'spread your legs for me' smile isn't going to work on me. I've seen it one too many times," she snapped at me, hands on her hips.

She was any guy's wet dream, but with a snarky mouth like hers, it was probably best to stay the hell away. I didn't need to add shit to my plate for the few days I was going to be in town. Or at least that's what I told myself as I opened my mouth to do the exact opposite.

"Can I at least get your name?"

The smirk that appeared across her face made it clear that this was going to be a fun game, even if it was one I shouldn't be playing. Then again, banter could be good, it didn't have to be anything serious. "Now why would I do that? Then you would have me at your beck and call."

Deliberately letting my eyes wander down her body. "What would give you that impression?"

She pulled a towel from her back pants pocket and wiped her hands on it. "Oh, so you're not like every other guy who walks through that door looking for a quick fuck?"

Chuckling, I shook my head. It had been a while since I'd felt this relaxed with another person. "Well, that's where you're wrong. I came in for the food I heard all about. The fact that the bartender looks like you is just a plus."

Rolling her eyes at me, she stepped up to the counter, handing me a menu. "Alright then, since you're here for *food* what can I get you?"

After a quick scan, I closed it and set it on the bar. "I think I'll have the Ryan burger special," I said, looking up into eyes that were a mix of blue and gray.

Her smirk turned into a slight smile. "That's a good choice. Anything to drink?"

"Sam Adams, whatever you have on tap."

Nodding, she walked over to the taps and picked up a clean glass, her eyes never leaving mine. The number of times she'd done that was obvious when she didn't need to look down to see when the glass was full. She set the glass in front of me. "I'll bring your order out when it's ready."

"Thanks."

The beer went down smoothly just like I knew it would. It was exactly what I needed. This was just the beginning. It was a good thing the motel was in walking distance. My stomach started to rumble, reminding me I hadn't eaten since this morning when I left the last motel. This was where I probably would have stopped for lunch and kept on my way. Since I was stuck here, I was going to make the most of being able to sit back and not have to worry about finding a job. I had enough saved up for more than a week without having to worry about working to replace it.

It wasn't long before the brunette returned with my meal and, holy shit, did I choose correctly. The burger was huge and smelled amazing. It barely fit in my hands when I picked it up, but the first bite was worth it. With how hungry I was, it didn't take me long to finish it. Ironically the brunette didn't stray far from where I was sitting. It seemed as if all her talk was just for show. Every time I looked away from the TV, I caught her watching me. And each time she averted her eyes and pretended to do something behind the bar. By my third beer, I noticed that I was starting to watch her as well. It had been a little while since I fucked someone as hot as her and even though she made it clear that it wasn't happening, I still found myself fantasizing about what she would taste like when I licked right through the folds of her wet pussy.

There was yelling that interrupted my thoughts. When I looked up I realized that I'd lost sight of her. Scanning the bar I saw that it was her yelling at two guys. One was at least as big as me, the other a little smaller. The big guy probably had about fifty pounds on me. Her face was flushed and she ordered them to leave over and over again. Against my better judgment, I stood and made my way over to where the assholes kept on pushing.

"Is this shit really necessary?" I asked standing behind the guys.

Without warning the smaller of the two turned, fist raised and threw a punch at my face. At that moment, all the fights I'd been in since I struck out on my own were going to come in handy. I was able to duck, forcing him to swing into midair. What I didn't take into account was the beefier guy being able to move as quickly as he did, landing a shot directly to my ribs.

"Shit," I grunted, grabbing a hold of my side. It was a pretty good possibility that they were bruised, but that really wasn't what I had to worry about. If I didn't get the upper hand, these two were going to kick my ass.

"Tony. Brandon. Knock it the hell off," the bartender screamed, as I came up swinging, cutting my fist across the face of the beefy dude. Just as fast two arms wrapped around my body, in an attempt to pin them down. I was able to use the leverage and throw my body weight back enough to kick the guy in front of me in the stomach, sending him flying to his ass.

Unfortunately that threw us both off balance and we ended up crashing into a table, and onto the floor. I heard the glass break below me as my head slammed to the floor, but it wasn't until I felt the trickle of blood down the side of my face did I realize that it had cut a spot near my eyebrow. The adrenaline deadening the pain.

It was only a brief moment to wipe away the blood, yet it was enough for one of them to get their arms around me again, while his buddy kicked his foot into my ribs.

"Tony!" the bartender screamed, as she tried to grab the smaller guy around the waist to keep him from kicking me again.

It was enough to give me the chance to flip my fist back into Brandon's face. Not a full punch, just enough to get him off of me. Getting to my feet, I ignored the blood dripping from the cut above my eye. Pulling my arm back, I let my fist slam into his nose.

"Motherfucker," he screamed. Blood flying everywhere, I was pretty sure it was broken. An arm slipped around my throat, pulling me back and just as quickly it was gone. When I turned I saw the reason why. Kaden had the other guy in a head lock.

"You, assholes, again? How many more times are we gonna do this before you two idiots get the hint?" He shoved his hand into the guy's face, dropping him to the floor with a broken nose to match his buddies.

"Son of a bitch," Brandon cursed, covering his face with his hands in an attempt to stop the bleeding.

"We're not leaving until we get what we came for," Tony said with a muffled voice.

"Oh you're leaving alright," the bartender announced. "That is unless you want me to let these two beat the shit out of you some more while we wait for the cops to come." She looked back and forth between the two of them. "Now listen very closely, this is the last time you screw with my business. The next time you show your faces through that door, I'll have the police here to pick you up."

"Should I show them the door?" Kaden asked.

"Definitely," she said watching as both of the idiots were forcibly removed from the bar by Kaden.

With the distraction now gone, the pain in my ribs and head were becoming more uncomfortable. Miraculously there was a chair still standing that I sank down into. That was when I noticed the rest of the people in the bar standing around and watching. *Why oh why was this shit always happening to me?* Most of the time I had no problem staying out of other's people's shit. Then there were those times that my conscience roared to life and put me in situations like this. Places that I didn't need to be.

Taking a deep breath at the frustration with myself, the pain seared through my side. "Shit."

"Oh my god. I'm so sorry," the bartender came running over with a towel in her hand and pressed it to the cut over my eye to stop the bleeding.

Not wanting to draw in more air than I needed, I simply nodded.

"You alright man?" Kaden asked walking over to where I was sitting.

"I've been better. Who were those assholes?"

"*They* were the dipshits I bought the bar from a few years ago. It was—" the bartender started to say.

"Wait...you're Ryan?" I stumbled over my words. I expected the owner to be a guy as I'm sure everyone else did as well. The woman standing in front of me did not fit the stereotype of a bar owner. Although by now I should have learned my lesson about stereotypes. Most of the time, they weren't true. Especially in my case.

"That's me, but with two n's at the end," she said, sounding slightly exasperated. "I'm not surprised you thought I'd be a guy, most people do. I'm used to it by now."

She tilted my head back and removed the towel from my head. Pushing her fingers around the cut, caused me to flinch, sending a sharp pain through my ribs. I gritted my teeth to keep from yelling out.

"This is going to need stitches," she said. Standing, she turned to face the rest of the room. "Alright everyone, go back to your dinners. We'll have this mess cleaned up in no time." Turning towards the bar, she looked over at a taller blond behind the bar. "Jimmy, can you grab a couple of guys to help you get this cleaned up while I take..." She looked down, waiting for me to fill in my name.

"Ryder."

"...Ryder to the hospital?" She looked around at Kaden. "Do you think you could help me get him into my truck?"

"No problem," Kaden said, taking a step towards me.

"I'm fine," I said getting to my feet. "I just need to..." The room began to spin and I grabbed the back of the chair for support.

"Yeah, real fine," Ryann said, grabbing ahold of my arm. "You're coming with me."

A hospital bill was not something I had the money for at the moment. "Just take me back to the motel to lie down. I'll be fine."

"Come on you're going to the hospital." She leaned over to whisper in my ear. "Don't worry about the bill, I'm taking care of it."

It was like she could read my mind. I wasn't sure if that made me more comfortable or uncomfortable. Either way, I nodded knowing that I probably did need medical attention. Kaden and Ryann helped me out to Ryann's truck. This was the second time that I'd needed help with something and Kaden had to help me out. I didn't trust very easy, so it was interesting to find myself willing to accept help from strangers once again.

CHAPTER 3

The waiting room was crowded, but since the cut was still bleeding they took me back fairly quickly. Which was good because I was starting to feel a little fuzzy. The doctor performed a few tests and determined that, not only did I have bruised ribs, but I also had a mild concussion as well.

Just fucking great.

"You'll need someone to stay with you for the next twenty-four hours," the nurse said, while filling out my discharge paperwork. The doctor had already stitched up the cut and left the room. I wasn't going to argue with her about staying with someone. If I told her that I was staying in a motel by myself, she probably would stop me from leaving and admit me.

"Do you have someone to drive you home?" she asked.

"Yeah. In the waiting room. They drove me here earlier."

"Good. You also shouldn't be driving for the next twenty-four hours either."

"Not a problem," I agreed, squinting against the bright lights. At the moment, all I wanted was to get out of there and sleep.

She handed me the forms to sign and a paper that had all of the instructions for the next few days. Thankfully they used the type of stitches that would dissolve so I wouldn't have to come back later to have them removed. As I got up from the exam table, the nurse helped to steady me when I was having difficulty getting my bearings. She forced me to sit in a wheelchair, saying something about hospital policy. I could only guess, based on my looks, that she thought I would argue, but I was too tired to give a shit. The sooner she got me to the waiting room the sooner I could get back to my room and lie down. Pushing through the double doors, I saw Ryann and Kaden waiting for me. Immediately they came over.

"How is he?" Ryann asked the nurse, who looked at me for confirmation that she could reveal any information. I nodded not wanting to waste energy on speaking.

"He has a mild concussion and bruised ribs. He'll need to be monitored for the next twenty-four hours for additional symptoms. If you see anything on the list of things I've given him, bring him back in." Except, I hadn't wanted the nurse to tell her that part. I just knew what was going to come next.

"We'll take good care of him," Ryann agreed. "Kaden, do you think you could pull up the truck?"

"Yeah, no problem."

She handed her keys to Kaden and looked back at the nurse. "He'll be staying with me."

A couple minutes later, I saw Ryann's black Chevy 2500 pull up right outside the exit. "I'll wheel him out to the car," offered the nurse.

I was sure she told me her name, but for the life of me I couldn't remember what it was. Whatever her name, she wheeled the chair out through the exit to the waiting truck. I was still having trouble standing, so Kaden hopped out and came around to help me in the truck. Once we were all in and pulled away from the hospital, I looked back at Ryann, even though it made me dizzy to turn my head that fast, I did everything I could not to let it show.

"You guys can just drop me off at the motel. I'll be fine, I just need some sleep."

Ryann scoffed. "Um...no. You heard what the nurse said, you need someone to stay with you."

"I did, but I'll be fine."

"The answer is no." She leaned up from the back. "Kaden why don't you stop by the bar and grab your truck, then meet me at my house?"

"Sure." He shrugged and turn to look at me. "There's no point in arguing with her."

"Yeah, I'm starting to figure that out," I said turning back around to lean my head on the cool glass of the door. The numbing medication was starting to wear off and my head was beginning to throb. Before I could continue the argument about where I was staying, my eyes drifted shut and I fell asleep.

When I woke up again, it was to Kaden and Ryann helping me up a set of stairs that definitely did not lead to my motel room. "Where are we?" I asked, my words sounded slightly slurred.

"My house," answered Ryann. "I told you in the car you weren't staying alone. You couldn't even stay awake long enough to argue with me. So forget the grief you're about to give me. Keep your mouth closed and we'll have you set up in the guest room in no time."

I wanted to argue with her, but it just felt like too much effort. All I wanted was to sleep and from what it sounded like, that option was only a few more steps away. We moved down the hall to the first room on the right. Ryann opened the door, letting me pass by, using Kaden as support. Ryann pulled down the covers and they helped me into the bed.

"Go to sleep," Ryann ordered. "I'll check on you later."

Unable to keep my eyes open any longer, I closed them and let myself drift off to sleep. I could deal with everything else later.

I hear pounding on the door.

"Open the door, Jonathon. You have some explaining to do."

Looking over at the clock, I realize that it's the middle of the night. Groaning, I throw my legs over the side of the bed. I keep my door locked so my brother can't get in. After what I found, I don't trust him at all. Trudging over, I flip the lock. Before I have a chance to reach for the handle the door crashes open, almost hitting my face, but I am able to jump out of the way in time.

"What is this?" my father roars at me, holding up a sheet of paper that looks very familiar.

I take the document out of his hands and instantly recognize what it is. "This is the paperwork I gave you earlier to prove my suspicions about David."

"Oh really?" he sneers. "Then how come the more I dig into this the more the evidence points to you and not your brother."

That isn't right, I'd checked and double checked to make sure I was right. David is the one, not me. The paperwork should show how much money David has stolen from the company, leaving the retirement fund almost bankrupt. I wouldn't do that to my family.

"I'm not sure. He must have done something to change it."

"I don't think so. You're always looking for a way to bring him down, to make yourself look better than you are. This is just another example of that. Except this time you actually caused our family a world of pain and suffering."

How can he accuse me of that? I've done everything I can to help and protect my family.

"Dad, I would never do something like that."

He takes a step towards me. "Don't lie to me. You've always wanted to be better than your brother, but you could never measure up and you never will. Yet you concoct this scheme to get your brother in trouble. You have always been the trouble maker."

Trouble maker? I'm not the one that pushed my brother out of my life. I've been there for him since he was born. For some reason, he pushed me away years ago.

"Dad, I swear to you on my life that I didn't do it."

"Right. And I'm supposed to believe a sniveling little rat like you, who only ever looks out for himself. You could never be half the man David is."

What did I miss? When did my father start to hate me? We were never particularly close, but he always showed me that he loved me and cared. What the hell has happened over the last few months?

"David is the cause of all of this. I've worked my butt off for you—"

A hand wraps round my throat cutting off my air, as I feel the wall slam against my back. A pain sears down my side and I can't get a breath. Eyes the color of my own look at me with hatred and a desire for murder flashing in them. My whole body starts to shake, only making the pain stronger. My father has never laid a hand on me before tonight.

He swings and his fist connects with my jaw, snapping my head sideways. The pain in my ribs forgotten, I flip my knee up landing a direct hit to his balls. Letting go, he doubles over in pain. Scooting around him, I reach the door only to find my brother waiting for me on the other side.

Not once in my life have I raised a hand to my brother, but I know that this is not the same David I grew up with. So before he can stop me, I swing my fist connecting with his jaw. While he's stumbling back and before my father stands up, I grab my jeans, a shirt, and shoes.

Thinking quickly, I realize my wallet is in the car. With my clothes in hand, I run down the steps, ignoring the calls of *my mother behind me. No matter what, I have to get away from the house until I can prove my innocence, since right now David has created enough falsified documents to have me arrested and thrown in jail for years.*

Yanking my keys off of the counter, I run to my car, leaving everything I know behind me.

"Ryder," a voice yelled next to me, startling me out of the dream.

My eyes snapped open, searching around the room. There was nothing familiar about it, but that was normal for me. *Where the hell am I?* I sat up, realizing instantly that was a bad idea. My head spun so fast, I felt like I drank an entire bottle of cheap whiskey. Then again, the pain in my ribs whenever I took a breath far outweighed any discomfort from my head.

"Lie back down, you're going to make it worse."

My eyes looked for the source of the voice. A beautiful brunette was sitting next to me on the bed. Her blue eyes were full of concern.

"Where am I?" I asked, completely confused as to how I got there and why the hell I felt like shit.

"My place. You don't remember the fight."

"Not exactly. If I did, do you think I'd be asking?" I knew I sounded like a dick, but I couldn't control my reaction when I was in pain.

"You don't need to be an asshole. I'm trying to help."

"Then don't give me ridiculous answers."

"Whatever. You have a mild concussion, which I'm going to use as the excuse as to why you're being a dick at the moment, and a set of bruised ribs."

I closed my eyes at the frustration. My brain was so fuzzy. "And what did I do to deserve those, this time? The last thing I remember was my bike breaking down and Kaden giving me a lift. He dropped me off at the motel, I showered, changed, and went to grab something to eat."

"At least you remember something. You came into my bar for dinner when those two assholes showed up again. When things got loud you tried to intervene and the jerks threw the first punch. Eventually you got the upper hand, but not before the damage was done. Kaden and I took you to the hospital when you were having trouble standing up and breathing."

I had a few little flashes of what she was talking about but nothing concrete. "Well, that sounds like it makes sense, except for the me getting involved part."

"And what's that supposed to mean?" Her voice got a bit louder.

The sound made my head throb even more. I cradled my head in my hands. "Please don't yell."

She sighed. "Why don't you go back to sleep. We'll talk more in the morning when your head's clear."

Figuring the pain would go away with sleep, I agreed and lay back down. My eyes closed and I was back into a dreamless sleep in no time.

When I awoke later, the sun was up and I was alone in the room. Flashes of the night before paraded across my mind.

Parts of the fight, a visit to the hospital, and then Ryann waking me up in the middle of the night. Surprisingly, I could remember her name when most everything else was one big blur. But for some reason I was able to remember my dream, maybe because it wasn't exactly a dream. Just the thought of the last time I saw my father made my blood run cold. The look in his eyes before he let me go and I fled the house for the last time still haunted me. It had been a long time since the memory assaulted me at night, but the concussion probably had something to do with that. Groaning, I threw my legs over the side of the bed, I needed to go find Ryann and get the hell out of there. I could hide in my motel room until the part came in and just order delivery.

I looked down and my shirt was missing, but I still had on my pants from the night before. A search around the room produced nothing. Frustrated, I left the room and went to look for Ryann.

CHAPTER 4

The smell of coffee led me downstairs to the kitchen where Ryann was sitting at the small table with a cup in front of her and another waiting at the empty seat across from her. Her eyes roamed from the top of my chest down to my abs, flinching when she took in the bruises on my side. Letting her eyes wander back up, she looked me in the eye.

"I heard you up, so I poured you a cup of coffee. I assume you drink it?" she said, gesturing to the cup already sitting on the table.

"Yeah," I said, dropping into the chair. "What happened to my shirt?"

"It was covered in blood, so I took it off you to wash it. Unfortunately, it didn't come out. I'll get you a new one."

"It's fine. I just need you to take me back to the motel."

She scoffed. "That's not gonna happen. You're stuck with me for the next twenty-four hours."

"Wh—" I started to yell before I realized how much it made my head pound. Lowering my voice I tried again, "What?"

"I guess you still don't remember much from last night?"

I went to shake my head and thought better of it. "Not really."

"You have to be monitored for the next twenty-four hours." She looked over at the clock on the stove. "Well, I guess fifteen hours. Until later tonight you aren't going anywhere without me."

This woman was going to make me crazy. "I'll be fine on my own. This isn't my first time with a concussion."

She rolled her eyes at me. "All the more reason you need someone to watch you and make sure there are no lasting symptoms."

"Why do you care anyway?" I groaned.

She looked down and watched as she swirled her coffee around in her cup. "It's my fault you got hurt in the first place."

"Not exactly, it's mine for getting involved. What did they want anyway? I know you said they use to own the place, but if they sold it, then it doesn't make any sense that they'd be bothering you."

She sighed. "The bar they sold me was a bankrupt piece of shit. They had no choice to sell it 'cause they didn't have the money to run it anymore."

"Okay. Well, of course you would sell something you couldn't afford."

"Yeah, but it doesn't end there. I bought the bar five years ago and worked my ass off to ditch the stigma the place had from them. Their food was inedible, the service was sucky, and the drinks were expensive. So no one would bother with it.

Took me a good two years to get people to start coming back into the place on a regular basis."

"That still doesn't explain what they wanted."

"The bar is successful now and they think I owe them more money. In their warped, twisted, little minds, they feel that since I got a deal on the place because of the condition it was in I should pay them more now that I'm making more money."

"That's really fucking stupid."

"Tell me about it."

"Why haven't called the cops."

"I have and they both have restraining orders on them. Not like that helps. Usually Jimmy calls Kaden when they show up and they throw them out."

This time, I guess it was my turn. I should have just let her handle it. In the end it would have been better for me. At that point, it didn't matter, what was done was done.

"Ryder?" she called a little louder.

I looked up. "Yeah, sorry. I got lost in my thoughts."

"You mentioned that you shouldn't have gotten involved," she said, crossing her arms over her chest. Getting up, she grabbed her cup and walked over to place it in the sink. A few moments passed before she turned around again, eyes blazing. "So why did you help then?"

I answered the question honestly. "I don't know, I just felt like I should." Watching her argue with those assholes didn't feel right. There was no denying she was beautiful, but from the moment I first talked to her, I enjoyed her spark. That "fun, I'm not taking no shit attitude" and to watch two obvious morons try to bring her down, set me on edge.

"You just felt like you should. Ryder, you're a very hard man to understand."

It wasn't that hard. I just chose to not let anyone in. People couldn't be trusted. They always screwed you in the end anyway. And the main reason I tried not to get involved—the closer you got to people the more it sucked when they fucked you over. When I didn't respond, she shook her head.

"Look, I'm going to get a shower. There's another bathroom upstairs and Kaden already grabbed your things from the motel. It's all in the bathroom."

My head snapped up. *Bad idea.* "He did what?"

"The room key was in your wallet. You tried to help me last night and got hurt because of it. I can't let you pay for a motel room. You can stay here until your bike is fixed if you want."

"What makes you think I'm not a crazy serial killer?"

"Because crazy serial killers don't help damsels in distress, and they certainly don't have nightmares that they wake up from with tears in their eyes."

My mouth dropped open. I didn't know the dream was that bad. When my father held me against the wall, I remember crying, but I hadn't let a tear drop over him since that moment. I forced myself to focus and found her on the stairs. She was about halfway up when she turned.

"Oh and there's aspirin in the medicine cabinet too."

With that she turned again and left me alone. It was weird, already she'd seen more of me than anyone else had in a long time. And the strangest part was, I didn't have the desire to run yet. I wasn't sure staying here until my bike was done was a good idea, although I knew there was no way she was letting me out of her sight for any length of time, at least until tonight. Resigned to that fact, I let the promised warmth of a shower call my name. I got up slowly not wanting make the dizziness worse. Once I had my balance, I tackled the stairs, holding my side to try and dull the pain in my ribs. True to her word, right at the top was a bathroom with my saddle-bag already inside.

The shower and aspirin were exactly, what I needed. However, getting dressed was not an easy task. Not that I was going to let Ryann know, or she'd try to keep me here until everything healed. It took me longer than normal, even pulling my shirt over my head was excruciating. When I finished dressing, I slowly made my way back down the stairs, where I found Ryann sitting on the couch. Damn. I stopped dead in my tracks. If the shirt from last night was low cut, there were no words for the pink halter top she was wearing. Even with the rest of my protesting body, I could feel my cock starting to harden. That was the last thing I needed. Giving myself a mental shake, I walked over to where she was sitting.

"Okay I'm showered and dressed, now what am I supposed to do with my day?"

"Well, I thought we could go get breakfast. After dealing with the bar every night I'm not usually in the mood to cook during the day."

"Alright. What do you normally do for breakfast then?"

"Depends on what time I get up. Sometimes breakfast turns into lunch. But since I went to bed pretty early for me and got up early, there's a great diner on the other side of town."

Now that the pain in my ribs and head was down to a dull ache instead of a throbbing, stabbing feeling, I was starting to get hungry. "Sure."

"Let me just grab my keys and we'll go."

We walked out to the garage. Watching the door lift, I wasn't surprised by the car sitting inside. It was a 1967 Shelby GT Mustang that fit her personality perfectly.

"Nice car," I said, walking inside the garage and running my hands along the perfect paint job.

"Thanks. My dad helped me fix it up."

"What about the truck?"

"I drive it to the bar and around town for errands, but whenever I can I take this baby out for a spin," she said patting the roof.

"I can't say I blame you. Does your dad live in the area?"

"No. He's still back on the east coast. Delaware to be exact." She unlocked the doors so that we could climb in. When we were both seated in the car she turned to look at me. "Where are you from?"

"A little bit of everywhere," I answered vaguely.

She pulled out of the garage and onto the road. "Were you parents in the military?"

"Not exactly."

"Do you wanna be more specific?"

"No, not really." There wasn't much to tell. Where I was born wasn't my home anymore. For me, home was wherever I slept.

"Okay then." Reaching over she flipped on the radio. The rest of the drive to the diner was made in complete silence except for the music from the radio. It wasn't exactly uncomfortable, just strange. Although, I could tell she was pissed with my lack of sharing.

The diner was farther than I expected, but if the smells from the outside were any indication, it would be worth the drive. My stomach growled. I hadn't realized how hungry I was. We were seated almost immediately in a booth in the back corner of the place. Since we'd walked into the diner, I'd only gotten hungrier. At least the menu looked good. After a few minutes of trying to decide, I closed the menu and placed it on the table. Once the waitress finished taking our orders, I noticed that Ryann was staring at me.

"I don't think you're as 'bad boy' as you pretend to be."

"And what makes you think that."

"I don't know there's just something about you. Something that tells me you hide behind the bad boy image, but deep down that's not who you really are?"

She was so spot on that I had to play it off. "What are we on one of those talk shows where I tell you all of my feelings?"

"See? That's you covering up. Trying to pretend you're the big bad biker." Her hand reached over to cover mine, her eyes catching and holding mine. "I know that's not who you really are. You don't need to pretend with me. I'm not going to tell anyone."

Watching the way she looked at me, made me feel more at ease than I had been in a long time. For some reason I wanted to open up to her, not everything, because some things were just too dark, but I wanted to share some things about me. I flipped my hand over in hers and began to caress the top of her hand with my thumb. It felt so natural to do.

Without taking my eyes from her, I started to give her pieces of my story. "I grew up in Connecticut. My family owns a pretty big business there, but I haven't talked to them in long time. Since I left, I move around from place to place, not wanting to stay to long and letting people get to know me. I don't trust people and it's why I normally don't get involved in other people's problems."

"Yet here you are helping me and telling me about your life. Why?"

"I have no idea. I've asked myself the same question. While I usually don't trust people, there is something about you that I do."

She smiled, a beautiful smile that shocked every part of me. It brought out things in me that I hadn't felt in a long time. But I was going to do my best to avoid exactly what my dick wanted to do. A good, quick fuck was one thing when it was with a nameless someone you didn't give two shits about.

When it was someone you saw differently, a person who you could tell would mean more to you, it was a whole different thing entirely. Especially when you couldn't explain why you felt more comfortable around a person you had known less than a day, than with people you had known for years or even months. That was it, I had to stay away from her. She deserved better than to be screwed over by a guy like me.

Throughout breakfast she asked me more questions about myself. Nothing as personal as earlier. Things like what kind of work I did and why I picked my bike.

"So tell me how old are you?" she asked putting the fork to her lips.

I was having a hard time concentrating as slide the fork out of her mouth. Forcing myself to focus, I answered her question.

"I'm twenty-six. What about you?"

"I'll be twenty-five in a month."

"How did you meet Kaden?" It was a question, I'd been dying to ask since my brain started to function again. Here I was secretly lusting over a woman that could have a boyfriend that helped me twice already. Wouldn't that suck.

"Kaden's my older brother."

"Brother?"

"Yeah, he beats me by little over a year, but he likes to pretend he's still in charge of me. Especially since Dad lives thousands of miles away."

"You said Dad. Where is your mom?"

Her eyes stared off into the distance. "My mom died of cancer when I was seven."

"I'm sorry."

She shook her head and smiled. It was overly bright and not remotely real. Just like I hid my scars, so did she. She wanted me to think that everything was okay, but I could tell that there was that seven year old girl, somewhere inside her, who missed her mother more than she was willing to admit.

After a few minutes of silence, she spoke up again.

"Where were you headed when your bike broke down?"

"I was heading onto Edgewood. Hoping to find a decent job there."

"Oh, the city. Not a fan of small towns."

"No, not really."

"Fair enough. What are you going to do when you get there?"

"I'm a tattoo artist. As soon as I find a job, the owner of the last shop is going to ship my guns and supplies to me."

Her eye traveled down my arms, the same time her tongue snaked out wetting her bottom lip.

"Why am I not surprised?"

That one action alone had my cock straining against the zipper of my jeans. God did I want to touch her.

Overall it was the best meal I'd had with company in a long time. The problem was that the concussion was making me tired again and I was having a hard time getting my dick under control. We paid the bill, I refused to let her pay my half. When she tried to argue that it was her idea to go out and eat, I had to remind her that I would have eaten out anyway since I was staying at the motel. That soothed her a bit and she agreed to us both paying half.

When we got out to the parking lot and she stopped to unlock my door, the view of that tight ass in front of me was more than I could handle. When she stood straight again, I spun her around and captured her lips with mine. There was a moment's resistance on her part, then she let go and let her lips slide against mine. Her taste alone could drive a man crazy. A heady combination of mint and vanilla. It was intoxicating. The moment her tongue slid out to touch my lips I groaned. Ignoring the pain in my side, I pushed her back into the car and continued to devour her.

The feel of her hands as they slipped up my, around my neck, and into my hair had me pressing myself closer to her body, letting her feel the how much my body wanted her. Craved her. She was passion, fire, and sweet wrapped into an irresistible package and I wanted more. My hands were braced on the car, pinning her between it and me, when someone cleared their throat behind me and giggled. It was like a bucket of ice water was dumped on us. She turned away at the same time I took a step back. We were both watching each other, panting for our next breath, which did not feel good in the least. But the memories of her warm lips went a long way to banish the pain. That didn't mean that I didn't feel bad for seducing her in the parking lot.

"I'm sorry, I shouldn't have done that."

Her breathing was still labored. "No that's okay. I'm worried about your ribs." Her voice was huskier than before. Without another world she stepped around me and got into the car. Without the adrenaline of the kiss, the exhaustion crept in.

She drove us back to her house and forced me to go upstairs to lie down. If I hadn't been so tired I may not have listened. Then again I wasn't really in the mood to deal with Kaden either. She threatened to call and have him come over and escort me to bed if I didn't listen to her. Apparently their relationship was how a normal sibling relationship should be. It explained a lot about why he was willing to step into the fight when no one else would and knowing that he would do anything for his sister, I didn't want her dragging him over here to put me to bed. I needed to deal with what happened in the parking lot, but I was way too tired to try and think. Upstairs I went and just as quickly as I closed my eyes, I was sound asleep.

CHAPTER 5

My eyelids drifted open to see that it was getting dark out. Even though it was fall, it was still pretty warm outside. I went down stairs in search of Ryann. When I couldn't find her, I looked at the clock on the stove. It was after five. Ryann had gone back to the bar for the night. When I turned, I noticed the note sitting on the table for me.

Ryder,

Sorry, I didn't want to wake you, but I had to head over to the bar and get everything up and running for the night. I'll bring you something for dinner later. Relax, watch TV, make yourself at home. Snacks are in the drawer and stuff to drink in the fridge. Cups are in the cabinet to the left.

Ryann

Was she running from the kiss earlier? Was that why she left me the note? Nah, she didn't seem like the type to run from her fears. With the way she demanded I stay and rest, it seemed pretty reasonable that she would have wanted me to sleep as much as possible. Yet, she left me here alone, after telling me that she was watching me for the next twenty-four hours. That's when I heard the key in the door and Kaden came striding into the living room.

"Hey, man," he said cheerfully, a slight laugh to his voice. "I'm here to be your babysitter until Ryann gets back."

I rolled my eyes. "You've got to be kidding me. Hasn't she figured out yet that I'm gonna be fine?"

"Nope and I'm not telling her that. If you haven't noticed my sister's temper gets out of control when she's mad."

Well, that was true. "Fine, whatever. I was about to grab a drink and then watch some TV until she gets back and releases me from her charge."

"Yeah, I don't think that is going to happen anytime soon, so you might want to get used to being here until your bike's done." He laughed, the smug bastard actually laughed.

Although I didn't want to say it out loud, I completely agreed with his assessment of the situation. Plus, since I had my tongue down his sister's throat only a few hours earlier, I didn't want to end up on the wrong side of Kaden if and when he found out. Luckily my errant cock was under control. I could only imagine how Kaden would react if he noticed the hard on I had for his sister. Grabbing two bottles of water out of the fridge, I handed one to Kaden and we sat down in the living room. There wasn't a lot on the TV, but I had so many things on my mind that it was hard to concentrate on much.

Since the pain in my head was better, I let Kaden choose the show and let my mind wander to earlier in the day. I still couldn't believe how much I told her, or how comfortable I felt with her. Or that I fucking kissed her after I decided to keep my hands to myself. Everything was weird. Here I was, this stranger who she now had staying in her house, all because I didn't want some fuckers to yell at her. There was nothing about this that made sense. And then I had to go and put my hands on her. It was like an addiction, one taste and I wanted so much more. At least an hour passed as we watched TV in silence, me still confused about everything. I wanted answers and maybe from Kaden I could get some more insight into his sister

"Why does it matter so much to her?" I asked Kaden.

He looked away from the TV. "Why does what matter so much to her?"

"Why does me staying here mean so much to her? I mean she just met me, it just doesn't make sense."

His eyes searched the room, looking everywhere but at me. I could just tell I wasn't going to like the answer, but without my bike it wasn't like I was going anywhere soon. The tension in my shoulders didn't bode well for my patience.

"Kaden? What the fuck is going on here?"

He stood up and was looking down at me. "Relax man. She didn't want me to tell you. She was pretty sure you'd flip your shit, which is what you are about to do."

Fuck. Did she tell him what happened earlier? Maybe not, either way it was irritating as hell to be told what to do. Then there was that part of me who hoped she wanted me to stay because of me. Don't ask me where the hell those thoughts came from.

"So explain it to me."

"I don't think I should."

"Are you kidding me?" I yelled and grabbed my side, when I sucked in a lung full of air.

"Don't get all worked up, man, you're just going to hurt yourself."

"What do you expect? I'm trapped here with no way to go anywhere without my bike and the only two people I've met in the city are fucking hiding things from me." I jumped to my feet. My pulse was pounding in my ears and I was having trouble controlling my temper.

"Fine, she heard you talking in your sleep last night. That's all I'm gonna say, if you wanna know the rest ask her."

"Ask her what?" a voice floated through the doorway. It was low and sexy. Damn, stupid dick was hard, just by the sound of it."

My head snapped around to see Ryann standing there, looking extremely fucking hot. Even as pissed as I was, my dick hardened to the point of pain.

"Exactly what you heard me say last night..."

Her eyes bulged out of her head, but she covered it quickly, taking the bag of food she brought into the kitchen first. Following her, I crossed my arms over my chest waiting for an answer. I heard Kaden's footsteps right behind me, I was sure it was an attempt to protect his sister. Little did he know, I would never hurt her I just wanted answers.

"Ryann, what the fuck is this all about?" I asked in a deadly, calm voice.

She looked up from placing things on the table. "Kaden, thanks for coming over. We're good."

"Are you sure? I can stay if you need me to."

Without taking my eyes from hers, I watched as she looked up over my shoulder at Kaden. "We'll be fine." Her tone left no room for argument.

"Alright, call me if you need anything." His footsteps retreated until I heard the door open and shut.

"Ryann—"

She put her hand to stop me. "Can we eat first?" she asked gesturing to the food on the table.

I made no move toward the table, arms still crossed over my chest waiting. When she realized that I wasn't giving in, she threw her hands up in the air.

"Fine. When you were having that nightmare last night, I heard you begging your dad to stop, swearing that you didn't steal anything."

Shit. I never let anyone know about it. That's when I saw the look in her eyes and what I saw there made him want to punch a wall. Pity. It was written all across her face. One thing I never wanted from anyone was pity. Everything I had at this point, I'd earned on my own.

"So all of this," I gestured around the kitchen. "This is all about pity. The kiss, was that pity too?"

"No, but I wanted to help."

"You wanted to help," I yelled. "I'm a grown fucking man who doesn't need help or pity." I turned heading for the stairs. The reason I kept to myself was staring me straight in the face. Never in all the time since I left my parents' house did I want pity for what I lost. I'd survived on my own without any help.

"Ryder, wait," she said catching up to me.

I kept walking. "I'm fucking out of here."

"But what about the concussion?" she asked panic clear in her voice.

"I'm fine." Reaching the top of the stairs, I threw everything into the saddle bag, tossed it over my shoulder, and made my way to the door.

"Where are you going?"

"Back to the motel."

"Please stay."

I turned around to look at her. The sadness in her eyes, cooled some of my anger but not enough to stay. "No. The next time you pick someone to 'take care of' make sure that's what they want."

With that I turned around and walked out into the night. I was so fucking pissed. Here I was fantasizing about a woman who only pitied me. To think that I told her more than I told anyone else bothered me a little, but not enough to go back. Ryann didn't live far from the bar so it was only a few extra blocks to get back to the motel. I stopped at the pharmacy on the way there to grab some aspirin for my head. When I got back to the room, I lay down on the bed, hoping that the part for my bike I was waiting for arrived soon. I needed to get out of this town. The sooner, the better.

My stomach growled and I realized I hadn't eaten since this morning. Picking up the phone in the room, I called the front desk for a number for a pizza place that delivered. After what happened the last time I went out in this town I wasn't taking any chances.

A while later, after the pizza was gone and I was lying in bed, letting my head rest, I made some decisions. There was no more moving for me. Once I got out of this town and found a place in the city I was staying put. All of the traveling and problems along the way were getting to be more than I wanted to deal with. I wanted a place to call my own; a place far enough away from all of the bullshit that seemed to follow me everywhere. And no matter what I was going to avoid Ryann at all costs. With that decision made, I let my eyes close in hopes of a dreamless sleep, afraid that my body would want to dream about her when my mind knew it had to stay the hell away.

CHAPTER 6

Two days later, I was still waiting for the part. I hadn't heard from Kaden or Ryann, which was good, except I wanted the call from Kaden that the bike was done and I could get on my way. Either way, I was becoming a bit stir crazy. There wasn't much to do in this place, and I wasn't feeling exactly adventurous to go out and explore. I was waiting for the pizza place to deliver the cheesesteak I ordered when there was a knock at the door. Thank god, I was freaking starving. Opening the door, I wasn't expecting what I found.

"Ryder, can we talk?" Ryann stood there, her red top enhancing the slight flush of her cheeks and a black skirt that accentuated her long shapely legs. As hard as I tried not to look, my cock was more than interested.

"There's not a whole lot to say." I was doing everything I could think of to keep my cock under control. "Thanks for taking care of the bills. I'm fine. You don't need to worry about me."

She pleaded with her eyes, and in the outfit she was in there was not much I could do to resist her. I nodded and gestured for her to come in. Shutting the door behind her, I waited as she walked further into the room.

"Well?"

"I came to apologize. I get why you were pissed, but I wanted you to know it was more than that." She fidgeted with her hands, but her eyes stayed on mine. "I noticed you the moment you walked into the bar. It was fun playing around with you and until those two dickheads showed up, I was ready to keep up our banter for the rest of the night. I wanted you to push until I finally agreed to have a drink or dinner or whatever you might offer. Then you kissed me the other day and my whole world flipped. You see, I wanted to spend more time with you, before any of the other things happened. Everything else just made me realize that you aren't the bad boy you pretend to be. And I want so much to find out who is under the exterior you put up for everyone else."

This had to be some kind of fucked up dream. I wanted her that first night. Who wouldn't? She was fucking gorgeous. Then after the kiss in the parking lot I wanted her so much more. The fact that she was standing here, telling me how much she wanted me was a fucking turn on. Then I thought about what a turn on that no nonsense personality was. Just when I thought my dick couldn't get any harder it did. It was why I intervened in the first place when the guys came in. The reason I was willing to share more about myself than I had with anyone in years.

Without letting myself think about what I was doing, I walked over to her and used my fingers to lift her chin so I could capture her mouth. The first taste of her lips on mine sent shivers down my body. I claimed her as if I had the right to do so. She was so responsive, wrapping her arms around my neck, threading her fingers into my hair. The same as the other day and it set my blood on fire.

My hand snaked down her body to the bottom of her skirt and skimmed back up her thigh until I reached the front of her thong. The warmth of my hand as it slipped around to cup her ass sent tremors through her body. It had been awhile since I had a woman as beautiful as Ryann in my arms.

Sliding my fingers back through her core, I pushed her thong to the side so I could slip my finger through that warm, wet sanctuary my body yearned for. After stroking a few times, but never touching her clit, my finger slipped deep inside her and thrust in and out. Her hips began to move to the rhythm I'd created. Groaning, I withdrew my finger from her body to grab the hem of her shirt and pull it over her head, exposing her lacy red bra that left little to the imagination. The nipple rings in both breasts were well defined under the fabric. Wasting no time, my hands went to the zipper on the back of her skirt, and with a quick flick of my wrist, it fell to her feet. I sucked in a breath, my gaze roaming over every part of her exposed form and stopping at the long expanse of toned skin peeking above the boots she still wore. Desire masked the pain from my ribs.

Slowly I lowered myself to my knees, needing to taste her. Using my tongue I traced a line at the top of the fabric. With little nips down her stomach I reached her inner thigh, sucking on the skin there. The noises coming from the back of her throat made me harder than I ever had been. Kissing my way back up, I used my teeth to lower the thong until it reached the top of the boots she was wearing. Finding the zipper on her boots, I made quick work of her footwear. My teeth returned to where they left off bringing the thong down past her knees. All the while, I was running my hands over any of the exposed skin I could find.

At the most inopportune moment there was knock on the door. The food.

"Shit. Give me one minute beautiful."

The blood rush to her face as she stepped to the other side of the door to hide. Wrenching open the door, I grabbed the sandwich and handed the kid a twenty, telling him to keep the change. I shut the door so hard, it rattled in its frame. I turned back to see Ryann grabbing her clothes. "I'll leave you alone so you can eat."

Setting the sandwich down on the nearest flat surface, I walked towards her, determination in every step and took the clothes from her grasp.

"Aren't you hungry?"

"Oh I'm hungry, just not for food." I wrapped my hand around the back of her neck and pulled her lips to mine. Kissing her until her body melted back into mine. The feel of her small hands at the hem of my shirt and I knew that I couldn't rest until I had her. The shirt was pulled up over my head and dropped to the floor. Once she did that, I stepped back and sunk to my knees to admire the goddess that was before me.

There she stood in the middle of the room, looking like a feast for a starving man. I took her hand and helped her step out of the thong, throwing it across the room. Sitting back on my heels, I watched her with a look of admiration and lust in my eyes.

"You're fucking gorgeous," I said and released an appreciative sigh.

I leaned forward and placed my tongue along the base of her core. "You taste amazing, too."

Her hand fisted in my hair along the back of my head.

"Ryder?" she whispered, and my eyes snapped to hers. "Please touch me."

I didn't have to be asked twice; my hands reached up to cup her ass, while my tongue continued to tease her sweet spot. Trembling, she moaned with satisfaction when my tongue flicked out once again, this time rubbing over her clit. I felt the tremble in her legs and feared that she may not be able to stand much longer. I stood up, swept her into my arms, and carried her over to the bed. Before crawling up her body, I rid myself of the rest of my clothes, stripping faster than I ever had in my life. Using my elbows, I held my body weight above her, I leaned up over her and took her lips with mine.

Heat flushed her cheeks red, but I continued. "I need to get rid of this bra." Reaching around her back, I flicked the snap on her bra with one hand. The sight of her pierced nipples was almost my undoing. My body surged with need.

Combined with the hibiscus tattoo snaking down her ribs, she made for an overly erotic sight. Lowering my head, I licked around her nipple, eventually sucking the little ring into my mouth, tugging until she let out a little gasp.

Lifting my head, I looked down at her. "Too much?"

She shook her head, taking deep panting breaths. "No. Please don't stop."

Unable to deny her body or mine, I lowered my head to her other breast, lavishing it with the same attention. At the same time, I let my hand snake down her body until my fingers found her clit, tracing circles over the top, causing her head to thrash fitfully on the pillow while she made soft whimpers.

When I couldn't take anymore, my head so dazed with passion, her body close to its peak, I moved my lips down her skin to where my fingers had just been, licking up and down her folds and eventually taking her clit into my mouth. My tongue swirled around it and lightly sucked, driving her mad. The beauty of watching her as I worshipped her body with my mouth was almost more than I could handle. My eyes focused on her as her breathing became more labored with each pass of my tongue, but her world exploded when my tongue thrust deeply into her. The thrusts of my tongue continued as I helped her ride out the aftershocks of her orgasm.

Taking my time, I nibbled a path up her body, making sure to stop and pull each nipple ring between my teeth. When I reached her lips, I lowered mine, taking possession of hers once again. With the first swipe of my tongue her lips opened to the wildly erotic kiss. My lips moved down her neck to suck a hot, wet path across her chest, reaching her breast, I sucked her whole nipple into my mouth, causing her back to arch off the bed. The torture of touching her was combination between pleasure and pain.

"Ryder, I need you now," she begged between labored breaths.

My tongue licked out to swirl around her nipple never touching. "Not yet."

The torture for both of us continued. But I wanted her to come again first. Sucking her clit into my mouth was the proverbial straw, her body arching off the bed, coming for what seemed like hours. My mouth moved back to hers as I settled between her legs, my dick stroking her pussy but never entering her. Her head thrashed on the pillow.

"Ryder, fuck me."

Groaning, I plunged full length into her. "Oh my God, you feel so fucking good," I groaned into the curve of her neck.

It was too much. I needed to get my body under control, or this would be over way before I wanted it to be. Ryann thrust her hips up trying to get me to move. Throwing my head back, a muscle twitched in my neck as I fought for control. The passion was so much that the dull throbbing in my head was easy to ignore. "Please don't move, unless you want this to be over before it truly starts," I hissed between clenched teeth. I sucked in a deep breath fighting the demands of my body.

Once I was in control, I began to take deep, driving strokes, bringing her back to the edge. Her nails dug into my back, holding me tighter to her as her insides started to clamp around me. She was close, which was good, because so was I. The feel of her, the constriction was all too much. When she crashed over the edge tightening her grip on me, I lost it. Pumping harder in the midst of her orgasmic bliss, I felt the tingle race up my spine and I let go, coming so hard I could have blacked out from the pleasure.

My body collapsed against hers, no longer able to hold myself up. Slowly our breathing returned to normal. I moved to her side, pulling out of her. Ryann rolled over and lying her head on my chest, her hands tracing my abs in a sleepy caress. With no energy left, we both fell into a deep exhausted sleep.

I was too warm. The air conditioner was running, but why was I so hot? That's when I remembered the woman sleeping next to me.

What had I done?

I leaned up on my arm looking down at Ryann. She was beautiful, the sex eclipsing anything from my past, but I was too damaged. I didn't want or need anyone's help and Ryann needed to help people. She was everything I wasn't. Now I just wasn't sure what I was going to do.

Quietly and with as little movement as possible, I slipped from the bed when my phone buzzed on the desk where I left it.

Kaden: Part's in, bike will be done in about 15 min. Should I come get you?

I thought about if for less than a second before I replied.

Me: No. I'll come to you.

I didn't want Kaden coming here to find his sister in my bed, especially since I planned on leaving. Grabbing a piece of paper from the desk drawer, I wrote her a note. With a brief glance around the room, I decided to leave the note on the nightstand where she was sure to see it when she woke up.

No matter how pissed I was yesterday, she had been kind to me. There hadn't been a lot of that for me in a long time. And while she deserved to hear it directly from me that I was leaving, I just couldn't do it. Ryann was the kind of girl who was going to haunt my dreams. There was no doubt about it.

The saddle bag felt like a heavy weight on my shoulders as I turned towards the door. With one last look at her, I left, shutting the door without a sound. The trip to the shop was pretty quick even being on foot. When I got there, Kaden had my girl outside, ready and waiting. She looked beautiful, just like freedom always did. Yet, that time there was a tightness in my chest at leaving.

Kaden walked out of the garage, wiping his greasy hands on a rag. "She's all ready to go."

"How much do I owe you?" I asked.

"Don't worry about it. My sister and I caused you enough trouble while you were here."

"You don't have to do that. Look, man, I'm sorry about what happened yesterday."

"Don't be. My sister has a way of stirring up her own trouble." He held out his hand to me. Taking it, I gave him a nice, firm shake.

Pulling the saddle bag off my shoulder, I got it connected to the back of the bike.

"Any ideas on where you're headed?"

Like sister, like brother. Always looking for more info. "The city. A place where I can be a face in the crowd."

I straddled the bike and turned the key to start it up. She purred beautifully. Picking up my helmet, I looked over at Kaden once again. "Thanks for everything."

"No problem. Good luck." He waved.

Pulling my helmet over my head, I grabbed the handle bars and drove out of the parking lot. The feel of the wind blowing around me had always brought me comfort as I took to the road. This time, though, I felt like I was leaving a little part of me behind. Images of Ryann flashed through my mind. Her standing behind the bar giving me shit, the way she sat at the diner and got me to open up, the feel of her lips against mine. It didn't matter. Leaving was for the best, I was too damaged, too emotionally distant for someone like her, I tried to convince myself as my bike put miles between me and her.

Read the continuation of Ryder and Ryann's story in
Second Chances coming in 2015

ACKNOWLEDGEMENTS

Thank you to my family. Your constant support means the world to me. I love you all more than you could ever know.

Missy, you are amazing. Ryder needed the love and care that you gave him. I'm super excited for our future endeavors.

To my beta readers, thank you for sticking with me and your patience with my crazy self.

Brandy, I love our daily chats. Thank you for all of your help with the cover for Ryder. Having the confidence to do that myself is all thanks to you.

Miranda, I know I'm super crazy but thank you for putting up with me anyway.

To my BFFs, I'm so glad I've gotten to know you all. It's super exciting when I get to meet you at signings and I love hanging out with you all. We can do anything we put our minds to.

ABOUT THE AUTHOR

Rebecca Brooke grew up in the shore towns of South Jersey. She loves to hit the beach, but always with her kindle on hand. She is married to the most wonderful man, who puts up with all of her craziness. Together they have two beautiful children who keep her on her toes. When she isn't writing or reading (which is very rarely) she loves to bake and watch episodes of Shameless and True Blood.

Facebook
www.facebook.com/pages/Rebecca-Brooke-Author/

Twitter
@RebeccaBrooke6

Website
Rebeccabrookeauthor.blogspot.com

Made in the USA
Middletown, DE
13 July 2015